Julia and McKinley's Day at the Beach

To Scarlett

K. Rebello

Kevin Rebello

AuthorHouse™
1663 Liberty Drive
Bloomington, IN 47403
www.authorhouse.com
Phone: 1-800-839-8640

First published by AuthorHouse   7/29/2009

ISBN: 978-1-4389-7330-2 (sc)

Printed in the United States of America
Bloomington, Indiana

This book is printed on acid-free paper.

authorHOUSE®

Julia Brooke awoke to the sound of birds chirping in the tree outside her window. She rubbed her eyes and jumped out of bed, landing on the floor with a big thump.

She reached back for her stuffed animal dog, McKinley, and pulled him through the mountain of blankets that lay on her bed. It was Saturday morning, and Mom and Dad had promised to take them to the beach if it was a sunny day. Julia Brooke grabbed McKinley by the arm and said, "Come on, boy, let's look out the window and check the weather." She tugged on the shade and released it, sending it into a twirling spiral as if it were a slot machine. Her eyes grew wide as she saw the sun make its way above the house. "It's sunny, McKinley. We can go to the beach today. Hurray!"

Julia Brooke ran downstairs to get some breakfast. She loved cornflakes and milk with sugar sprinkled on it. She made herself a bowl and set up a pretend bowl for McKinley.

After breakfast, Julia Brooke ran into her parents' room to wake them. "Mom and Dad, it's sunny today! Can we go to the beach?"

"Sure, Julia Brooke," replied Mom. "We can go to the beach today. Why don't you take McKinley into the playroom and gather together all of your beach toys."

Julia Brooke headed for the playroom. She dug into her toy chest and started to take out all of the toys. "McKinley, don't just sit there, help me find the beach toys." So together, they dug through the toy chest one by one. "Here they are," proclaimed Julia Brooke after a few minutes of searching. "We have a rake, a shovel, a scoop, a sifter, a watering can, a blue pail, a red pail, a green pail, a trowel, and a sandcastle mold. Great work, McKinley! Let's put all of the toys in the beach bag."

Next, Julia Brooke opened the door of the linen closet, positioned her step stool, and climbed up so that she could reach the top shelf of the closet. She reached for a large beach blanket and some beach towels, pulling them off the shelf. She then opened the beach blanket so that she could see how large it was. Unfolding the blanket, Julia Brooke accidentally covered up McKinley. "Where are you hiding, boy? Yoo-hoo, McKinley … Where are you?" Julia Brooke lifted up the beach blanket and laughed when she realized what she had done. "There you are, boy. Come on, McKinley. We have to get to the beach!"

Julia Brooke ran to her bedroom, took out a purple bathing suit from the dresser drawer, and put it on. She then borrowed an old blue bathing suit from her dad and put it on McKinley. The bathing suit was a bit big for McKinley and covered up most of his hind legs. "You look funny in a bathing suit, McKinley," exclaimed Julia Brooke. She found two large brimmed hats for them, as well as some sunglasses and a pair of orange flip-flops. Now they were all ready for some fun at the beach.

Julia Brooke and McKinley headed for the kitchen to see what food Mom was preparing for their picnic at the beach. Mom was making a peanut butter and marshmallow fluff sandwich. Julia Brooke loved peanut butter and marshmallow fluff sandwiches, and she ate them every day for lunch. Mom also packed some strawberries, blueberries, watermelon to snack on, and orange juice and fruit punch to drink.

"Don't forget to bring some pretzels and oatmeal cookies," exclaimed Julia Brooke.

"Yes, little one," said Mom.

Dad packed up all of their beach supplies and loaded them into the car. The ride to the beach was only twenty minutes long, but because Julia Brooke was so excited to get to the beach, twenty minutes seemed like an eternity. To help pass the time, Julia Brooke made up a silly song and sang it out loud over and over again until they finally arrived at the beach. She laughed hysterically as she sang her song:

"Flisby floodle, jinx and droodle, rasty minamore. Sambatooty, winstiguty, mishka papadoor."

As they approached the beach, Julia Brooke could see the sand dunes and crabgrass from the backseat window of the car. She and McKinley couldn't wait to bury their toes in the sand. Dad parked the car, and they grabbed their toys out of the trunk and ran straight toward the water's edge.

There was a lot of room to run and play. Julia Brooke filled the sifter with some wet sand and pretended to make an apple pie. She fed a big slice to McKinley and pretended to eat a piece herself. "Isn't this the most delicious pie you ever had, McKinley?" she asked.

Julia Brooke laid McKinley down on a beach towel and filled her yellow bucket with sand. She dumped the sand on McKinley and repeated this several times until his body was completely covered except for his head. Julia Brooke didn't think that McKinley looked very comfortable buried in the sand, so she grabbed her shovel and began to dig him out. Once he was dug out, she brushed all the sand out of McKinley's fur and gave him a big hug. She was having lots of fun at the beach.

"Come on, McKinley, we're going to build a big sandcastle and let some sea creatures live in it." Julia Brooke gathered all of their beach toys and began to build a giant sandcastle. She filled several buckets with salt water, then packed some of the sand together using the sandcastle molds. McKinley watched as she mixed the sand and water together so that the sand coming out of the mold would stick together.

Julia Brooke constructed a large lookout tower, and she built a big wall around the tower to protect it. She then carved out a large basin in the sand so that the water from the ocean would flow all around their castle. When the castle was completed, it stood two and half feet tall. Julia Brooke and McKinley collected some beautiful shells along the shore and placed them in the sandcastle wall to make the castle look impressive. They were very proud of their creation.

Julia Brooke and McKinley were standing at the water's edge admiring their sandcastle when all of a sudden, a big wave crashed to shore. The wave caught Julia and McKinley by surprise, and they both fell down into the water. Even though they were soaking wet, it was so warm outside that the salt water felt really refreshing, so the two splashed around and laughed. When Julia Brooke helped McKinley get up out of the water, he had a large piece of seaweed on his head. Julia Brooke laughed and told McKinley, "You look like a giant sea monster!" She took the piece of sea weed off of McKinley's head and gave him a big kiss on his face.

The tide was rising, and seawater was filling in around the castle. Julia Brooke and McKinley constructed a large bridge over the water entering the basin of the castle using some long pieces of driftwood they had found on the shore.

Julia Brooke turned to McKinley and said, "We need to find some sea creatures to come live in our castle." The two gathered up their pails, shovels, and fishing net and started down the beach in search of sea creatures.

Julia Brooke and McKinley stood at the water's edge observing a school of silver fish swimming by. With one quick swoop of the net, Julia Brooke captured one of the shiny silver fish. The fish was frantically flopping around in the net. "Don't worry, little fish. We are going to bring you to our magnificent sandcastle where you can swim and live. My name is Julia Brooke, and this is my dog, McKinley. What is your name, little fish?"

"My name is Gil," replied the fish.

"It is very nice to meet you, Gil," replied Julia Brooke.

Julia Brooke looked over at McKinley and said, "Quick, we need to get Gil back to the sandcastle and place him in some water before his scales dry out." She grabbed McKinley by his paw and ran down the shoreline with the fishing net in hand. When she arrived back at the sandcastle, she placed Gil into the waterway that surrounded the sand castle. He was happy to be back in the water, and he began to swim laps around the sandcastle. McKinley and Julia Brooke headed down the shoreline once again to find some other sea creatures.

Julia Brooke looked under some rocks and spotted a beautiful red and blue hermit crab. She scooped the crab into her net and said, "Hello there. I am Julia Brooke, and this is my dog, McKinley. What is your name?"

The hermit crab replied, "My name is Shelley."

"It is very nice to meet you," replied Julia Brooke. "We are going to bring you to our magnificent sandcastle and put you in a room with a big rock and some seaweed in it. You can live in the sandcastle with our silver fish, Gil. I am sure you will love it."

Julia Brooke and McKinley ran back to the castle and placed Shelley in his special room. Shelley seemed happy with her room, and she immediately climbed under the big rock. Julia Brooke was so excited that her sea creature friends were enjoying the sandcastle. Again, Julia Brooke and McKinley headed back to the shoreline to find another sea creature.

As the two proceeded down the shoreline, they spotted several pink starfish clinging to the side of a rock. Julia peeled one of the starfish from the rocks and placed it into her red pail. "Hello there. I am Julia Brooke, and this is my dog, McKinley. What is your name?"

The pink starfish replied, "My name is Squirt."

"It is very nice to meet you, Squirt," replied Julia Brooke. "We are going to bring you to our magnificent sandcastle and put you in a room with lots of sand and small stones for you to hold on to. You can live in the castle with our silver fish, Gil, and our hermit crab, Shelley. I am sure you will love it".

Back at the sandcastle, Julia Brooke placed Squirt in his special room. Squirt immediately crawled over the stones and burrowed his body into the large pile of sand. It was difficult to see Squirt because he camouflaged himself with the sand.

Julia Brooke was happy to see her sandcastle filled with sea creatures.

Julia and McKinley watched for hours as Gil, Shelley, and Squirt played inside the sandcastle. Julia exclaimed, "What a wonderful castle! Now you sea creatures will never have to return to that big, scary ocean. You can live in our castle forever and ever!"

Just then, Shelley cried out, "I'm getting hungry, and I want something to eat."

Julia Brooke grabbed McKinley by the arm and ran up the beach to where her parents were sitting on a beach blanket eating lunch. She grabbed some of her leftover peanut butter and fluff sandwich and brought it back for Shelley.

Shelley said, "Thank you for trying to get me some food, but hermit crabs don't eat peanut butter and fluff sandwiches. We like to eat plants and grasses that live deep on the ocean floor."

Julia Brooke scratched her head and said, "I don't have any plants or grass to feed you."

Shelley replied sadly, "I'm so hungry! How am I going to get anything to eat if I stay in this castle?"

Julia Brooke was unsure how she was going to feed Shelley, and she felt really bad.

It was now one o'clock in the afternoon, and the tide was low. The ocean water that was once filling the pools in the sandcastle had stopped, and Squirt was calling for Julia Brooke. "My skin is starting to dry out, and I miss my family of starfish."

Julia Brooke got angry at Squirt for sounding so ungrateful and not relishing the sandcastle she and McKinley had constructed for her sea creature friends. She replied, "I will get you more water." Julia Brooke and McKinley grabbed a yellow bucket and filled it with water. They poured the water over Squirt, but within minutes the water had all disappeared into the sand. Julia was confused, "I don't understand", she said. "I have constructed this beautiful castle for my sea creature friends, and they are not happy living here."

All of a sudden, Julia heard the squawking of a seagull. The seagull was circling the castle and began to swoop down on Gil. Julia quickly grabbed her fishing net and shoed away the seagull before it could swipe him. Gil was frantic! "I want to return to the ocean," he said. "This castle is not safe enough for me, and I don't want to get eaten."

Julia Brooke did not know what to do. She grabbed McKinley and walked up the beach to meet her parents. She explained to Dad how the sea creatures no longer wanted to stay at the castle. Dad told Julia and McKinley, "I know that you both meant well by constructing a sandcastle for your friends to live in, but sea creatures belong in the ocean. Your friends need to live with their families just like the two of you live with Mom and me."

Julia Brooke looked at her father with a disgusted look, but then realized that Dad was right. Her sea creature friends needed to return home. Julia Brooke turned to McKinley and said, "We need to return our friends to their homes and families at once."

Julia Brooke and McKinley sprinted to the sandcastle. As they approached, Julia Brooke could sense how apprehensive her sea creature friends were. She looked at Gil, Shelley, and Squirt and said, "I'm very sorry that I took you from your homes and brought you to my sandcastle. McKinley and I are going to return you to your habitat."

The sea creatures were all very excited to go home. Julia Brooke grabbed her fishing net and placed Shelley and Squirt inside, and then put Gil into a bucket of water.

She brought the bucket to the water's edge and said, "Good-bye, Gil, you are a really good swimmer, and it was really nice to meet you." She dumped the bucket of water into the ocean, and Gil dove in, making a splash. Gil said good-bye to Julia and McKinley, then swam away to join the rest of the school of fish.

Next Julia Brooke and McKinley returned to the rock where Squirt's family was sunbathing with other starfish. Julia Brooke picked up Squirt from the net, and they said goodbye to one another. Julia Brooke could tell that the other starfish were glad to see Squirt return home.

Finally, Julia Brooke and McKinley returned to the big rock under which Shelley lived. Julia Brooke opened the fishing net and let Shelley out.

Shelley said, "Thank you, and goodbye." Then she headed out to find some plants for lunch.

Julia Brooke and McKinley were exhausted. They trudged up the beach to meet up with their parents. "I'm ready to go home," said Julia Brooke.

Julia Brooke missed her sea creature friends, but she knew that returning them to the ocean was the right thing to do. Julia Brooke and McKinley fell asleep in the back seat of the car with their head on each other's shoulder.

Dad patted their heads and said, "I'm proud of both of you."

Printed in the United States
154783LV00004B

9781438973302